The Other Side

JACQUELINE WOODSON ◆ illustrations by E. B. LEWIS

G. P. PUTNAM'S SONS ◆ NEW YORK

Library of Congress Cataloging-in-Publication Data
Woodson, Jacqueline. The other side / Jacqueline Woodson ; illustrated by Earl B. Lewis.   p. cm.
Summary: Two girls, one white and one black, gradually get to know each other as they sit on the fence
that divides their town. [1. Race relations—Fiction. 2. Friendship—Fiction. 3. Summer—Fiction.]
I. Lewis, Earl B., ill. II. Title. PZ7.W868Th 2001 [E]—dc21   99-042055 CIP ISBN 0-399-23116-1
19 20

For Elisabetta and Tashawn—J. W.

To my dear friend Fran Emery—E. B. L.

That summer the fence that stretched through our town seemed bigger.

We lived in a yellow house on one side of it.

White people lived on the other.

And Mama said, "Don't climb over that fence when you play."

She said it wasn't safe.

That summer there was a girl who wore
a pink sweater.
Each morning she climbed up on the fence
and stared over at our side.
Sometimes I stared back.
She never sat on that fence with anybody,
that girl didn't.

Once, when we were jumping rope,
she asked if she could play.
And my friend Sandra said no
without even asking the rest of us.

I don't know what I would have said.
Maybe yes. Maybe no.

That summer everyone and everything
on the other side of that fence
seemed far away.
When I asked my mama why, she said,
"Because that's the way things have
always been."

Sometimes when me and Mama went
into town, I saw that girl with her mama.
She looked sad sometimes, that girl did.

"Don't stare," my mama said. "It's not polite."

It rained a lot that summer.

On rainy days that girl sat on the fence in a raincoat.

She let herself get all wet and acted like she didn't even care.

Sometimes I saw her dancing around in puddles,

splashing and laughing.

Mama wouldn't let me go out in the rain.
"That's why I bought you rainy-day toys,"
my mama said.
"You stay inside here—where it's warm and
safe and dry."

But every time it rained, I looked for that girl.
And I always found her.
Somewhere near the fence.

Someplace in the middle of the summer, the rain stopped.

When I walked outside, the grass was damp

and the sun was already high up in the sky.

And I stood there with my hands up in the air.

I felt brave that day. I felt free.

I got close to the fence and that girl
asked me my name.
"Clover," I said.
"My name's Annie," she said. "Annie Paul.
"I live over yonder," she said, "by where
you see the laundry. That's my blouse
hanging on the line."

She smiled then. She had a pretty smile.

And then I smiled. And we stood there looking at each other, smiling.

"It's nice up on this fence," Annie said. "You can see all over."

I ran my hand along the fence.
I reached up and touched the top of it.

"A fence like this was made for sitting on," Annie said. She looked at me sideways.

"My mama says I shouldn't go on the other side," I said.

"My mama says the same thing. But she never said nothing about sitting on it."

"Neither did mine," I said.

That summer me and Annie sat together
on that fence.
And when Sandra and them looked at me
funny, I just made believe I didn't care.

Some mornings my mama watched us.
I waited for her to tell me to get down
from that fence before I break my neck
or something.
But she never did.

"I see you made a new friend," she said
one morning.
And I nodded and Mama smiled.

That summer me and Annie sat on that fence
and watched the whole wide world around us.

One day Sandra and them were jumping
rope near the fence and we asked
if we could play.
"I don't care," Sandra said.

And when we jumped,
Sandra and me were partners,
the way we used to be.

When we were too tired to jump anymore,
we sat up on the fence, all of us in a long line.

"Someday somebody's going to come along
and knock this old fence down," Annie said.

And I nodded. "Yeah," I said. "Someday."